ONE WINDY DAY

Copyright © 1990 American Teacher Publications
Published by Raintree Publishers Limited Partnership
All rights reserved. No part of this book may be reproduced or utilized in any form or by any means, electronic or mechanical, including photocopying, recording, or by any information storage and retrieval system without permission in writing from the Publisher. Inquiries should be addressed to Raintree Publishers, 310 West Wisconsin Avenue, Milwaukee, Wisconsin 53203.

Library of Congress number: 89-70333

Library of Congress Cataloging in Publication Data

Caraway, Jane.
    One windy day / by Jane Caraway; illustrated by Jerry Smath.

    (Ready-set-read)
    Summary: A cumulative tale in which various neighbors try to rescue Janey's kite from a tree until she has to rescue both the kite and the neighbors.
    [1. Kites—Fiction. 2. Neighborliness—Fiction.] I. Smath, Jerry, ill. II. Title. III. Series.
PZ7.C1860n 1990   [E]—dc20   89-70333

ISBN 0-8172-3579-5

1 2 3 4 5 6 7 8 9   94 93 92 91 90

READY·SET·READ

ONE WINDY DAY

by Jane Caraway
illustrated by Jerry Smath

Raintree Publishers
Milwaukee

One windy day, Janey's kite got tangled
at the top of a tall, tall tree.

4

Before Janey could do anything, along came the ice cream man in his blue truck. "I can climb the tree," he bragged. "I'll save the kite."

However, when the ice cream man reached the
top of the tall, tall tree, he looked down,
and that was a mistake. He was so scared,
he could not move a muscle.

6

The wind blew, the tree shook, and the branches bent. Now the ice cream man and the kite were trapped at the top of the tall, tall tree.

7

Before Janey could do anything, along came the principal on her yellow motor scooter. "I can climb the tree," she bragged. "I'll save the ice cream man and the kite."

However, when the principal reached the top
of the tall, tall tree, she looked down, and that
was a mistake. She was so scared, she could not
move a muscle.

9

The wind blew, the tree shook, and the branches bent. Now the principal and the ice cream man and the kite were trapped at the top of the tall, tall tree.

10

Before Janey could do anything, along came
five fire fighters in their red fire engine. "We can
climb the tree," they bragged. "We'll save the
principal and the ice cream man and the kite."

However, when the five fire fighters reached
the top of the tall, tall tree, they looked down,
and that was a mistake. They were so scared,
they could not move a muscle.

12

The wind blew, the tree shook, and the branches bent. Now the five fire fighters and the principal and the ice cream man and the kite were trapped at the top of the tall, tall tree.

13

"Whooooshhh," moaned the wind.
"Creeaakkk," went the tree.

14

"Aaaaaaaaaaahhh," cried everyone at the top of the tall, tall tree.

Now the branches of the tall, tall tree were
bent down almost to the ground.

16

"Quick," Janey said as she grabbed a branch. "Jump!"

When the five fire fighters and the principal
and the ice cream man saw that they were
close to the ground,

18

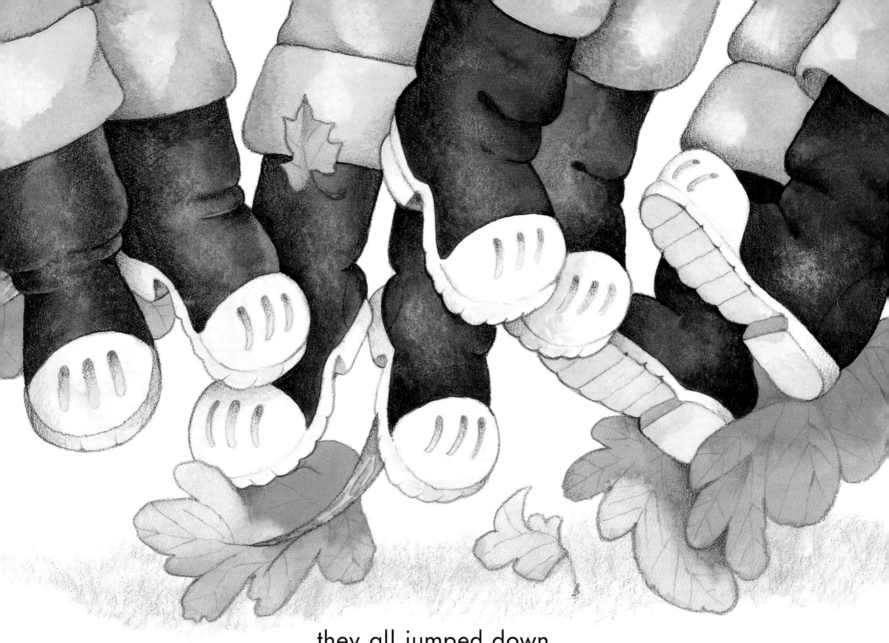

they all jumped down.

Kerplop!

19

Everyone laughed and hugged each other.
The ice cream man was so happy he gave out
free ice cream.

Everyone forgot all about the kite—everyone but Janey. All by herself, she climbed up to the top of the tall, tall tree and got her kite.

Then she climbed down and hurried off for home.

23

Sharing the Joy of Reading

Reading a book aloud to your child is just one way you can help your child experience the joy of reading. Now that you and your child have shared **One Windy Day,** you can help your child begin to think and react as a reader by encouraging him or her to:

- Retell or reread the story with you, looking and listening for the repetition of specific letters, sounds, words, or phrases.

- Make a picture of a favorite character, event, or key concept from this book.

- Talk about his or her own ideas or feelings about the characters in this book and other things that the characters might do.

Here is an activity that you can do together to help extend your child's appreciation of this book: You and your child can play a game to discover more about sounds. In **One Windy Day,** the wind goes "Whooooshhh!" and the tree goes "Creeaakkk!" Listen with your child for noises heard around the house, such as a door closing or a telephone ringing. Think of words that can stand for those sounds, like SLAM! or BRRING! You and your child can take turns as one person makes a sound for an object and the other person tries to guess the object.